NOUVEAUTÉS PARISIENNES
Le Bonnet de Paris
L'ULTIME COUVRE-CHEF

Miss Hunnicutt's Hat

By Jeff Brumbeau
Illustrated by Gail de Marcken

ORCHARD BOOKS
An Imprint of Scholastic Inc. • New York

For Lea Koplon, who has inspired me in ways I'd never imagined, and Ina Stern, who with a simple act of kindness gave me a life in books — J. B.

For Esther — G. de M.

LIBRARY OF CONGRESS CATALOGING-IN-PUBLICATION DATA
Brumbeau, Jeff. Miss Hunnicutt's hat / by Jeff Brumbeau ; illustrated by Gail de Marcken. p. cm.
Summary: Miss Hunnicutt is determined to wear her new hat adorned with a live chicken for the Queen's visit despite the disapproval of the other townspeople. ISBN 0-439-31895-5 [1. Hats—Fiction. 2. Assertiveness (Psychology)—Fiction. 3. Peer pressure—Fiction.]
I. De Marcken, Gail, ill. II. Title. PZ7.B82837 Mi 2003 [E]—dc21 2002004983

10 9 8 7 6 5 4 3 2 1 03 04 05 06 07
Reinforced Binding for Library Use Printed in Singapore 46 First edition, March 2003
The artwork is rendered in watercolor. Text type is set in 12-point ITC Esprit Medium. Book design by David Saylor

5

One fine day in the tiny, little town of Littleton, everyone was as busy as could be. The Queen was making her summer trip from city castle to country castle and would pass right through Littleton promptly at three.

No one really thought the Queen would stop at a little town like Littleton, because it was, well, just too little. But just in case, they'd be ready. Everywhere everyone was scurrying to paint the cottages purple, the Queen's favorite color. They were sweeping the streets and tying ribbons to the trees and turning out in the very best of their best.

All except for the timid, quiet Miss Hunnicutt. The celebrations for the Queen were all well and good, but Miss Hunnicutt always did her shopping on Tuesdays at three o'clock. Usually she didn't like to make a fuss and always did what everyone wanted her to do.

WHIMPLE
MILLINER
WELCOME
STOP FOR
Wolfenbuttel

But today, the day the Queen was to pass by, she decided to put her foot down. Well, hopefully. Miss Hunnicutt was going to do her shopping and wear her new hat from Paris, even if it was a little different.

Just before three o'clock, Miss Hunnicutt peeked from behind her door. She stepped outside and although she looked much the same as always, with her hair in a small bun, a canary-yellow dress, the same blue traveling coat and goose-head umbrella, there was something different.

That — was her hat.

It looked quite like the hats the other ladies of the town wore. It had blue felt and green and yellow ribbons, and great big feathers all about. What was different was that this hat had chicken feathers. And the feathers were still stuck to the chicken who was happily clucking away on Miss Hunnicutt's head.

Just then Mrs. McSnoot came marching down the street with her poodle.

"Why, Miss Hunnicutt!" shouted Mrs. McSnoot (she always shouted everything she had to say). "What on earth is on your head?"

"It's my new blue hat," she said in a tiny voice. "It came all the way from Paris. Oh, I do so hope you like it."

"Like it!" bellowed Mrs. McSnoot. "It's horrible! It's terrible! It's a chicken! You can't wear a chicken on your head!"

"Well why, why is that?" asked Miss Hunnicutt.

"What will the Queen think?" Mrs. McSnoot cried. "The second she sees that awful thing she'll drive right by! You must take it off this instant!"

"I just don't know," said Miss Hunnicutt in a tiny voice. "I think I might have the right to wear what I like. And I won't wear a lobster and I won't wear a weasel. But I would like to wear a chicken. And I'd like to wear it on my head."

"It has to go!" declared Mrs. McSnoot. And she poked her bony finger in the chicken's face.

Now the chicken, who didn't see very well and needed spectacles, thought her finger looked just like a worm. And so she bit down fast and hard.

"*Yowwww, owww, oww!*" Mrs. McSnoot wailed.

All of this shouting made the neighbors stop their work. The first was nosy Miss Bisbee. She and her cats stuck their noses out the door to see what was going on. Suddenly, Mrs. McSnoot's poodle broke away, dragging her along behind and running right between Miss Bisbee's legs and after the twenty-seven cats inside.

At first all was silent. Then twenty-seven cats with twenty-seven *meows* leaped through windows and doors and ran right up the old apple tree in the yard. Miss Bisbee skipped a jittery jig around the tree.

"Call the Fire Department!" she cried. "Call the Navy! Tell them my babies are up a tree!"

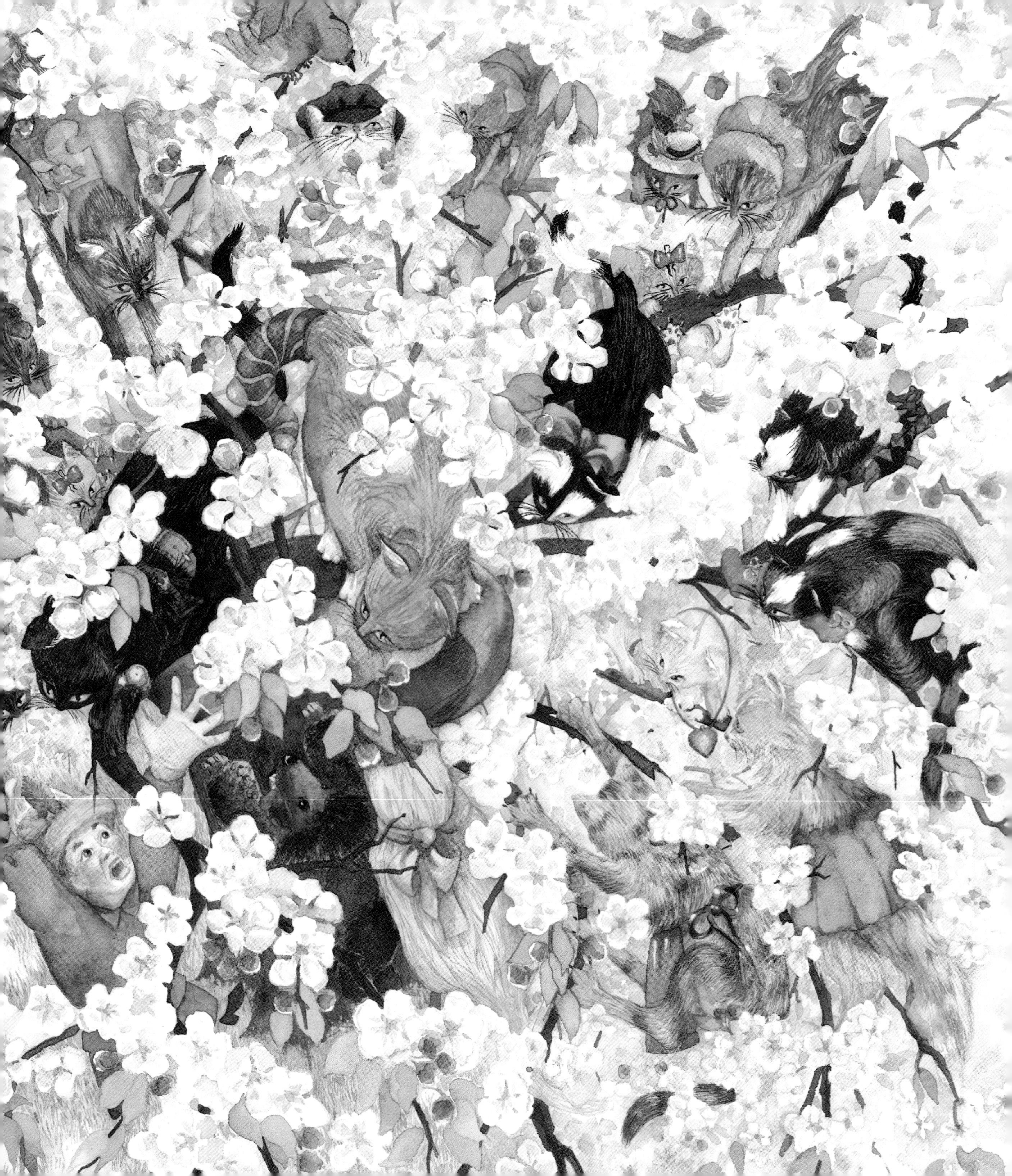

The Fire Department came right away. But just next door the ever nervous Miss Whimple was taking a bath. And so when she heard the fire truck's siren she just knew her house had to be on fire.

"Fire! Fire!" she screamed. Then she wrapped the shower curtain around herself and leaped out the window. Right into the Fire Chief's arms.

In Miss Whimple's hurry, she had forgotten to turn off the water. First one drop, then two, then a trickle, then a waterfall began to rush out the window. Soon mud was running from her garden into the road, and everywhere people were slipping and falling.

Now it should be said that the people of Littleton could be very stuffy. They believed that you had to dress their way or there was something wrong with you. And so when tales of Miss Hunnicutt's chicken hat spread throughout town, everyone hurried to gather around her.

Now all were as mad as they were muddy. The Queen was due any minute and everything was going wrong. *What else could happen?* they asked each other.

Mrs. Coriander, head of the refreshment committee, looked up at the courthouse clock and then down Piccolo Street. Sure enough, the baker's truck was coming with the twelve-foot-high cake. And the truck with the raspberry soda was coming from the other end of the street.

SODA

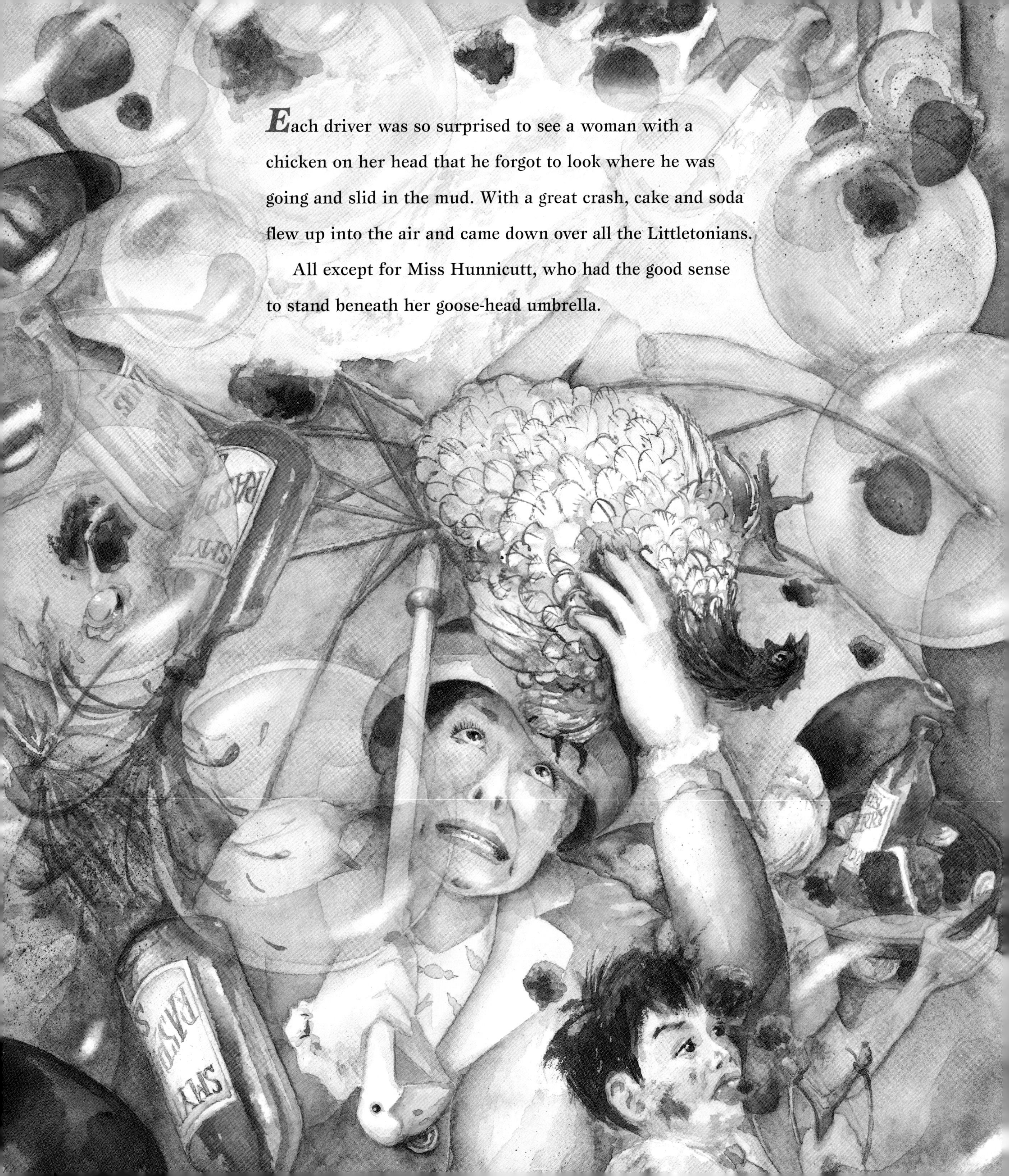

Each driver was so surprised to see a woman with a chicken on her head that he forgot to look where he was going and slid in the mud. With a great crash, cake and soda flew up into the air and came down over all the Littletonians.

All except for Miss Hunnicutt, who had the good sense to stand beneath her goose-head umbrella.

"Just look at us!" cried one in the crowd.

"What will the Queen think?" said another.

"She'll be here any second!" warned a third.

"It's all your fault! Take off your hat!" the crowd shouted at Miss Hunnicutt. "Take off your hat!"

"I — I don't think that I should," Miss Hunnicutt firmly said. "I'm pretty sure I have the right to wear what I like. And I won't wear a rhinoceros and I won't wear a poodle. But I'd like to wear a chicken, if you don't mind, and wear it on my head."

The crowd grumbled and groaned, but Miss Hunnicutt stood a little taller than before.

THE

Just then Mayor McTwiddle waddled over.

"What in heaven is going on here?" he cried.

"Look at her in that hat!" cried one.

"This mess never would have happened if she hadn't put on that horrible thing!" said another.

"Now Miss Hunnicutt," said the Mayor, "we can't have your hat laying eggs when the Queen comes by, now can we? That wouldn't do at all. Therefore, as the Royal Mayor of Littleton, I must demand that you remove that ghastly thing this instant!"

"I will not!" she replied in a voice that was now both loud and sure. "I have the right to wear what I like! And I won't wear a flounder and I won't wear an orangutan! But I will wear a chicken and I will wear it on my head!"

"It's an abomination!" the crowd shouted. "The Queen will laugh at us as she rides right by!"

The Mayor thought for a moment and, as he did at such times, he placed a finger on the tip of his nose.

"There must be a law against wearing a chicken hat, and if there isn't, well then there should be. Therefore I have no choice but to put you, Miss Hunnicutt, in jail."

This made her very mad indeed.

"You can't do that!" she cried.

"Just what do you mean by telling me what I can't do? Why, I'm the Mayor!" said the Mayor.

"What do I mean?" said Miss Hunnicutt. "I mean corncobs."

"Corncobs?" said the Mayor.

"Corncobs?" said the crowd.

"Corncobs," Miss Hunnicutt said again. "Every night exactly at eight Mr. Yadda likes to juggle corncobs in his polka-dot underwear."

"Yes, it's true," Mr. Yadda said reluctantly. He then took out six corncobs and began to juggle. And the children in the crowd clapped.

"Now Miss Bisbee," continued Miss Hunnicutt. "She talks to her cats like they're people and dresses them up in clothes. And they're very well dressed indeed.

"And you, Mr. Mayor—"

"Yes, yes, yes," said the Mayor. "But what on earth has this to do with you and your hat?"

"Well," said Miss Hunnicutt, "if you're going to put me in jail for doing something you think is silly, then you'll have to put the whole town in, too! Because, as you see, they're just as silly as me."

"Hmmmmmmm," mused the Mayor with his finger on the tip of his nose. "A good point. A very good point indeed."

Just then the courthouse clock struck three and a boy called down from the tower.

"Here she comes! Here comes the Queen!!!"

The Mayor rushed to stand at attention beside the road. Behind him was the Littleton Tuba & Tambourine Band, The Ladies' Snooker Club, The Gentlemen's Yodeling Society, and the townspeople.

And all the way in the back was Miss Hunnicutt and her chicken hat.

Everyone waved and hoorayed and hurrahed as the longest, blackest, shiniest automobile anyone had ever seen whooshed down Main Street. And just when it seemed as though the Queen was going to whisk right by as always, the auto suddenly stopped. Then seven royal guards leaped about like cats to help her out.

The Littletonians gasped at the sight of the Queen. She wore a purple velvet cape, a dress that seemed to be woven from threads of sunlight, and slippers covered with bits of fallen stars.

The Queen marched past the Mayor. She marched past the Tuba & Tambourine Band, The Ladies' Snooker Club, and everyone else until she stood before Miss Hunnicutt.

The crowd whispered and wondered how the Queen would punish her for wearing so hateful a hat. A minute passed and the Queen clapped her hands three times. The royal guards jumped into the auto, and everyone bent their necks trying to see what was happening.

At last they came out, grandly carrying the Queen's hat. The Littletonians could not believe what they saw. It was a red hat, with festoons of yellow ribbons and tiny pink roses. There was a little bow in front and a happily gobbling turkey on top.

With her hat properly in place, the Queen then spoke.

"My dear, that is a most glorious hat," she said. "Would you care to trade?"

Miss Hunnicutt looked her right in the eye. "I have the right to wear what I like! And I won't wear a platypus and I won't wear a wombat! But now that I think of it, I might wear a turkey, I just might wear it on my head."

With their new hats placed just so, the Queen turned to go. But before she did she had a word with Miss Hunnicutt.

"I'm having a little bash for the usual kings and queens of the world. Why don't you pop by?"

"That might be pleasant," Mrs. Hunnicutt replied. And the two new friends walked arm in arm to the longest, blackest, shiniest automobile anyone had ever seen, and drove away.

TAXI
WADDLEWORTH
DOT'S TASTY
EGG
BAKE SALE TODAY
McSnoot TEA GARDEN

In the months that followed, first ten, then twenty-two, then all the ladies of Littleton were seen wearing chicken hats of their own. Even the gents went about with a chicken style of their own.

Finally, the town settled down to calm and quiet.

Then one day, Miss Hunnicutt stepped outside her door to do her three o'clock shopping. She looked the same as always, with her hair in a small bun, a canary-yellow dress, and the same blue traveling coat. A goose-head umbrella was hooked on her arm in case of rain.

But today she wore her new hat that came all the way from Bombay. It was green with pink ribbons and bows all about.

And, oh yes, on top,
looking quite handsome and
content, was a very pleased
and grinning porcupine.